Max and Zoe

at the School Concert

by Shelley Swanson Sateren

illustrated by Mary Sullivan

raintree 🍃

a Capstone company — publishers for children

Raintree is an imprint of Capstone Global Library Limited, a company incorporated in England and Wales having its registered office at 264 Banbury Road, Oxford, OX2 7DY – Registered company number: 6695582

www.raintree.co.uk
myorders@raintree.co.uk

Text © Capstone Global Library Limited 2014
This British English edition published in 2020
The moral rights of the proprietor have been asserted.

Designed by Emily Harris
Production by Katy LaVigne
Originated by Capstone Global Library Ltd
Printed and bound in India

ISBN 978 1 4747 9065 9 (hardback)
ISBN 978 1 4747 9071 0 (paperback)

British Library Cataloguing in Publication Data
A full catalogue record for this book is available from the British Library.

Contents

Max and Zoe's class were

practising in the music room.

"Next, we will hear 'The

Garden Tune'," said Mrs

Lewis, their music teacher.

Henry and Ruby hurried to

the piano.

Max walked slowly.

"Why did I say I'd do this?" thought Max. "I'm rubbish at singing."

Henry, Ruby and Max stood next to the piano.

"All right, gardeners,"

said Mrs Lewis. "Sing your

best. The rest of you hum

like bees."

Quietly, Henry and Ruby

began to sing. But Max

couldn't.

His mouth was super dry.

The microphone slid out of

his sweaty fingers.

"I'll totally mess it up

tomorrow," he thought.

"Louder, trio!" said

Mrs Lewis. "Come on,

Max."

Henry and Ruby sang a bit louder. Max tried to sing a few words.

"They'll be cross with me tomorrow," he thought. "Everyone will laugh."

After school, Max sat by Zoe on the bus.

"I'm so nervous," he said. "I'm going to be sick."

"No, you're going to practise," said Zoe. "I'll help you."

Chapter 2
Practise, practise, practise

Zoe went to Max's flat

after school.

"Use your comb for a

microphone," she said.

"Ready? Go."

Max looked at the sheet
music. He began to sing.
Buddy covered his ears with
his paws.

"See?" said Max. "My
singing is terrible."

"Go away, Buddy!" Zoe said.

Zoe lined up some stuffed

animals. "Sing to them,"

she said. "But first, breathe

deeply five times."

Max did, then started

again.

"Louder," said Zoe.

"Pretend you're excited to

sing on stage!"

Max sang loudly but read

some words wrong.

"Keep going if you mess it

up," Zoe said. "People won't

notice."

Max practised more, but
the animals didn't smile.
That made Max feel extra
nervous.

"I have a better idea,"
said Zoe. She drew pictures
of smiling faces. Then she
taped them to Max's wall.

Max sang and sang
to the friendly faces. His
breathing slowed down. He
remembered the words too.
After Zoe went home,
Max kept practising.

"Among the bees, we're on our knees, we're digging in the dirt," he sang. "Among the bees, we're on our knees, we're in our gardening shirts!"

By bedtime, Max threw
the sheet music away. He
was ready.

Chapter 3
The trio

After lunch the next day,

the concert began.

On stage, the class sang

the opening songs. And then

it was time for the trio.

Max's heart beat fast. He took five deep breaths. Then he picked a very friendly face to look at – his mum's.

Mrs Lewis began to play the piano. Max opened his mouth to sing.

All of the words came out,

clear and strong! But Ruby

and Henry weren't singing.

Max sang alone for

the whole song. Everyone

cheered. Max bowed.

After the concert,
everyone got milk and
biscuits.

"I'm sorry I messed up,"
said Ruby.

"Me too," said Henry.

"It's okay," said Max.

"Everyone gets nervous

sometimes. Here, have my

biscuits."

"Really? Thanks,"

they said.

"Wow, Max," Zoe said.

"You sang a solo!"

"I'm so proud of you, Max," said his mum.

"Thanks!" said Max. "I'm proud of me too!"

"And I think that deserves another biscuit," said Zoe.

About the author

Shelley Swanson Sateren is the award-winning author of many children's books. She has worked as a children's book editor and in a children's bookshop. Today, as well as writing, Shelley works with primary-school-aged children in various settings. She lives in Minnesota, USA, with her husband and two sons.

About the illustrator

Mary Sullivan has been drawing and writing all her life, which has mostly been spent in Texas, USA. She earned a BFA from the University of Texas in Studio Art.

Glossary

concert a show put on by singers or a band

microphone a stick-like tool that makes sounds louder

nervous fearful or timid

practice doing something over and over again to get better at it

solo a piece of music that is played or sung by one person

trio a piece of music that is played or sung by three people

Discussion questions

1. If you had to sing a solo, duet or trio, which one would you pick? Why?

2. Max learnt some tips to help him feel less nervous. What were they? List some other tips that can help you relax when you feel nervous.

3. Were you surprised by the end of the story? Why or why not?

Writing prompts

1. Max does a lot of practising. Write about something that you have practised.

2. The story introduces part of the song "The Garden Tune". Write more lines to the song.

3. Max is nervous about singing. Write about something that makes you nervous.

Make your own microphone

What you need:
- toilet-paper tube
- black card (12 cm long and 8 cm high)
- sheet of tin foil (1 metre long)
- craft glue
- scissors

What you do:

1. Glue the black paper onto the tube.

2. Cut off any extra paper. This is the mic's handle.

3. Scrunch the tin foil into a ball. Make the bottom pointy. This is the microphone.

4. Put glue inside the top of the tube.

5. Stuff the pointy end of the foil ball into the handle. The top should be a round, silver ball.

6. Let the glue dry.

7. Then grab your microphone and sing your favourite songs.

The fun doesn't stop here!

We have lots more Max and Zoe adventures for you to enjoy!

Discover more books and favourite characters at **www.raintree.co.uk**